AF405540

to the reader,
 Thank you for reading. i appreciate it so much. it doesn't take much to be an author but a strong heart full of empathy. go for your dreams and don't hold back. with peace and love, enjoy this simple easy read.

-a.c bolan

ALTHE
A.C Bolan

CHAPTER ONE

It was 6:14 am, I hadn't slept a wink last night. It was the second of April and already it felt like we had leaped from winter to summer. I had spent the night staring at the ceiling and listening to music while imagining scenarios in my head with this dilf, Mads Mikkelsen. Mads Mikkelsen was a danish actor who did his job so well, I had just finished binge-watching
Hannibal a week ago and yet I found myself rewatching it again.
Picking up my phone and seeing that only 3 minutes had passed by, I decided to get out of bed. I would normally wake up later. But even If I hadn't slept a wink last night, I seemed to feel fine without the sleep, until I stood up. My legs felt as though all the blood had rushed down to my feet like if I had ankle weights.
In the kitchen, my dad was prepping his food for work.
"You should go back to sleep," he said,
"no, I'm not tired"
"Well, I cooked way too much food for work, so help yourself to it later," he said as he walked out the
door for work.
 My dad was a good dad but I didn't always think that until a year later after my parents separated. I
spent time with both parents. alone with them and got to know them more than I ever had. spending
more time with my aging mother made me realize she was only good at bringing me down and for the
longest she had manipulated me to think that my dad was the worst, in reality, she was the worst, manipulative with a victim mindset.

CHAPTER TWO

I was a journalism major at my community college. I wasn't smart enough by GPA standards to go from high school straight to a university. I was a good student up until 7th grade. the math to me became harder and I also started daydreaming way more in class at that time. but when I look back now I regret it. "we're going to have to dismiss you, Althea," said Mr.Secilly. Mr.Secilly was a counselor at the college who was almost close to no help at all. "you haven't been passing your classes, it's like you don't have the interests to be here" Mr.Secilly started up again. "well, can you explain?" he said, "well, I'm not really sure what I want to do, I'm not really sure what I want to be" I said, "well" he began his sentence, almost as he was mocking me, "if you don't know what you want to be, then why are you here?" I shrugged my shoulders, I really had no clue. Mr.Secilly sighed with disappointment, "well, I'm dismissing you for a semester, and hopefully by the time you return, you'll have clue about what to do." he said and then shook his hands up and down, signaling me to leave. I left knowing in my gut that by the time I was allowed to re-registered, I still would have no clue.

CHAPTER THREE

It'd had been about two weeks since the whole dismissal and I couldn't bring myself to tell anyone I had been dismissed or else they would feel right about all the predictions they had made about how I would fail. "you'll fail college because you don't speak", "even if its a community college, you'll fail, you don't have the smarts", "just you watch, you'll drop out." the reality is, I'm not sure, if I'm not smart, or if I easily get distracted. I had finished my last two years of high school with a program that allowed me to do school work from home and then turn it in, in person, one day a week. I had a few A's but mostly B's. "shouldn't you be at school? or video chatting with your professor for this online hee-bee-jee-bees?" my mom said. "I already did," I said. she looked at me suspiciously but then continued to drink her daily cup of instant coffee. my mom's boyfriend came to visit that same day, it seemed like he was always there. he was 24 while my mom was in her late 40s, I'm unsure why he was with her but all I could think of was that there must be something wrong with him for him to be dating someone like mom. he pours himself a cup of coffee and began to speak of the most basic knowledge, I guess he liked the compliments my mom gave him because no matter how kindergarten level his knowledge was, my mom always seemed to compliment him with, "you're the smartest man i know!" what a baffoon I thought and he looked like one too.

i had been looking for a job since I was dismissed from school. I had absolutely no luck. application after application and rejection after rejection. I was beginning to feel hopeless and usually, when I do, I begin to overthink and think horribly of my self-worth and value. "do you want to come to goodwill with me? the one on oswell?" my older sister stood at the doorway of my room. "sure, it's not like I need anything better to do." my sister Maya drove a 1997 Toyota car, the ac had worked when dad had bought it second hand but somewhere along the timeline, it just stopped, so being in her car in warm weather was hell---to make it even worse it had leather seats so my bum felt as if it might burn off. "ok, don't forget your mask" said Maya. A pandemic had occurred in early January starting in China, then spread to Europe and soon enough here. masks were mandatory and a way to protect yourself from catching covid. "let's go to this rack of shirts" Maya said, as she walked to the specific rack. I didn't bother looking, I just stood there awkwardly. I didn't see the point in shopping for clothes, everything in my life seemed like it was falling apart. "I'm going to walk around," I said to Maya, "ok," she said to me distracted by pressing every pretty shirt she found onto her body to see how it would look on her. walking around the thrift store, I wanted something to entertain me, something to help get my mind out of the dark pitch black hole it had fallen into full of thoughts. the thrift store was full of worn-out teddy bears, baby toys, and board games which missed a lot of pieces. the thrift store also had an electronic section but I'm not so sure how you could even call it that when it only had old computer keyboards and calculators. next to the electronic section, or so they call it that, was a bookshelf full of books. books that had been loved until they ended up here for a new home. I thought to myself maybe a book could do, to cheer me up and make me feel hopeful once more. I was an avid reader in elementary and when I reached 7th grade, I just altogether stopped reading. was it because of puberty or the little society of middle school? I scanned the books with my eyes, reading the spine of the books for their title and author when my eyes layed on "Just Kids by Patti Smith". "Just Kids" I read to myself in my mind, with that voice that we use in our silly heads. I thought by the title, she felt like a kid at the young adult age of 19 like me but soon I would discover, that wasn't the case. "I found what I want," I said to Maya as I walked up to her, "ok so have I? look at this shirt, isn't it cute?" she said while showing me a plain black shirt. "sure," I said and we walked to the checkout.

CHAPTER FIVE

I lay in bed on my back, it had been aching probably because of how much I slouch when I sit reading and I had been reading a lot. it turns out, Patti Smith was a poet, singer, author, and artist. it amazed me that she was all that. the book Just Kids, in a way, was a biography and yet also a love story. "Hey, we're going to Morro Bay. get dressed and will you please put that book down." I threw on some light-washed jeans and an oversized striped button-up and tied it in a knot in the front since it was too big. I filled my tote bag with my book, a sketchbook, and pen. "I'll sit by the window," I said as I walked quickly to the left back door. I loved to sit by the window for long drives, I could daydream or simply watch the trees disappear until there was no more and the only land. Morro bay was only 3 hours away and I had no clue, why out of the blue they had decided to go. the car was so shakey that I couldn't hold my book still to read, so I shoved some earbuds into my ears and listened to music while I fell fast asleep. we arrived at Morro Bay, I heard the seagulls laughing and the water roaring. "It's early, what should we eat?" said my brother-in-law Brandon, who was dating my sister Maya for almost 5 years. They met on Facebook. "You choose, I don't care," said Maya, even though she was extremely picky. We ended up at some restaurant called Thai Bistro and since we were in a pandemic, only outdoor dining was allowed and as I sat at a table I could hear the seagulls laughing almost like they were laughing evilly because they planned to drop their dirty doo-doo on my head as they always seemed to do. "Curry, I want Red Curry," I said to the waitress. Brandon and Maya ordered curry too. it was a first and I was shocked since I made curry at home for myself and every time I offered them some, they'd say, "no thanks. your food is always weird." the curry came, it was golden and not red as I hoped it would be, given the name on the menu but regardless it was delicious. we walked around Morro Bay and through many little shops and I eventually found a bookstore where I bought more books. I was becoming interested in reading and I felt the positivity of it. we went to a beach nearby the many shops, there were clams and starfishes on rocks and in the sand. I dug up gems, which later I would find and see they were just rocks that looked shiny in the sun due to the salt, I suppose. driving back home, we stopped at a gas station which seemed normal on the outside, and then to our surprise, it was retro-themed inside. I bought a dollar bill that had The Beatles on it instead of George Washington's face. My favorite Beatle lad was John Lennon, his cooperation in protesting really inspired me but according to TikTok, he was canceled, despite being dead for 80 years.

CHAPTER SIX

I brought a clam from Morro Bay, I was unsure whether it was alive or dead. how can you tell? how can I tell? I checked on it every day. it never opened, until one day I saw it had stuck its tongue out. it made me happy to know he was alive and that a part of Morro Bay, such a peaceful side of the ocean unlike Santa Cruz was with me. My phone rang, "this is your community college, we want to give you a chance so we can avoid dismissal altogether." I hung up. I couldn't go back, no, not yet. I still didn't know exactly what I wanted to be and yet, at 19, I felt as though my life was flying down through my fingers like sand. I felt I should have certain things accomplished by this age. All I had accomplished was getting into a community college where anyone could get into. your local old man having a midlife crisis, the hot dads, the nerds you thought could get a scholarship but surprisingly didn't and then people like, moi, me. ugly odd ducklings. the black sheep of both the family, friend groups, and school project groups. just that thing. "Want to go to the bookstore?" my dad asked me as I read my book. "Sure, I've been wanting some true crime books anyway." whenever we went to the bookstore, my dad would always sit on the benches by the magazines. he enjoyed taking me places. he thought it was good I was distracting myself and he was proud of me for being an enrolled student or so he thought I was. "There it is!" I said to myself, grabbing a copy of Helter Skelter, a true crime book based on Charles Manson. He had run a cult and brainwashed people. I sometimes wish a cult leader would come across me and ask me to join the cult, I just wanted to see if I was mentally strong enough to not get brainwashed. I liked everything dark and anything to do with dark psychology. I wanted to go into Forensics until I saw the required math courses. I always thought I could also be a Psychologist too--or a history teacher but those dreams seemed so far to reach. On the ride home, I began to contemplate my life with the twilight soundtrack playing in my earbuds.

CHAPTER SEVEN

"Glad you came to see me," said Mr.Secilly After contemplating my life in the car after a trip to Barnes and noble, I decided it'd be best if I at least met up with an educational advisor. "This is Samantha, she's an educational advisor. speak to her and she can help." he left us in his little cramped office. "so, how can I help?" said Samantha with a sweet smile, "I don't know what to do with my life. I came here thinking and feeling so sure that I wanted to be a journalism major but now it seems like, well, I don't." "hmm," she said as she looked at me with annoyance, "what drives you? what motivates you?" she asked me "I just want to help people, I want to make them know that I feel what they feel sometimes; sadness, happiness, I want to help people. I want to touch people emotionally." "so then, change your major to nurse, my time is up, i have another appointment." she walked away quickly into the hall filled with many offices. "So? did that help?" Mr.Secilly walked in with a snickers bar that he probably got from the vending machine, if he wasn't eating nuts, he was eating snickers. "no" I said. As I walked out of the counseling building, I walked straight to admissions. I paid what I had to pay, all my debt with the last of my grant money, and swore to myself that I wouldn't come back. I thought it was silly how I could only become one thing when I had so many interests, I dreamed of being many things. The only thing I'd miss was the dilf in my one class of English and his salt-n-pepper hair. He looked like Thomas Gibson from Criminal Minds.

CHAPTER EIGHT

Since I had quit school, as I completely dropped out. I hadn't slept, it's been a week, and wonder if it has to do anything with the fact that I haven't told my family. I curled myself up in a ball, the blanket covering my head. "I am a failure, I am, I am, I am." I don't know what came over me because that moment I got the urge to get ahead shaver and shave my head as Brittany Spears did. Dad had his hair shaver in the cubbie where we kept the towels. I was home alone, Dad wouldn't be home until later. I connected the Conair hair shaver into the electricity plug, "bzz bzz". it was so scary. slowly and then quickly, I shaved through my hair hoping to feel relieved of my feeling of failure. I looked like Caillou. if he had a buzzcut. I felt the same and ended on the floor crying. Maya came at 1 pm, she does so sometimes and sometimes she doesn't come at all. it's all unexpected. "What have you done?! you look hideous!" she shouted at me, I continued to cry and just lie there like a bag of potatoes, except I'm certain the potatoes are still much more beautiful than me. she took me to the emergency room, she didn't know what to do with me, so she took me there. "She doesn't need us, she needs someone else," the doctor said as he handed us a card with a name and occupation title of "therapist" under the name. "she isn't crazy," Maya said about me to the doctor, I couldn't say a word, I felt nothing. I felt done for. "you're right. she isn't but therapists aren't just for crazy people, that's an old myth." the doctor replied. before we left that cold, bright emergency room, my sister Maya filled and signed some forms and we headed home for the last 3 hours of the late-night and early morning.

CHAPTER NINE

i sat in a waiting room. The carpet was navy blue colored and the scent of the room was infused with hand sanitizer or rubbing alcohol. The walls had those hospital-like paintings of flowers and the magazines they offered you to read while you waited were horrible. "Althea?" I heard a man call, "yes?" I answered back, almost as quiet as a mouse but the room was so quiet and still that it seemed I had been speaking at a normal volume. Hugh Crawfard was the name of my therapist, he was tall and young. not what I had expected, I expected for an old man, someone that looked like Einstein. He was the opposite, he looked like an actor with his hair slit back, black, pitch-black the way blood would look in the dark, with his perfect smile that could belong to a toothpaste ad and he was only 27. I walked into the room where all the chats would happen and then he'd tell me how to fix myself. At least I hoped it'd be that easy. Two leather armchairs faced each other and we sat on each other's opposite--facing each other, the way the chairs were set up, meant I would be making plentiful of eye contact with my hot therapist, I wanted to cry and evaporate. "How do you feel?" Crawfard started up, "I feel fine" "If you were fine, if you truly felt that way, you wouldn't be here right?" "Right" I answered back flatly. He was right, I didn't feel fine, I felt nothing. I began to explain how I felt and how stressed I was for myself presently and for myself in the future, how I felt like a real nobody at my age. "I see," he said while dotting away in his brown leather notebook. "What you need is to go out more, experience things, go on a boat, go out to eat. see what you like and don't like also meditate somewhere quietly to hear your thoughts and acknowledge them." I sat across from him, hearing him talk, I had nothing back to say and with my buzz-shaven head, I had nothing I could say. I already looked so crazy. I agreed with him. he walked me out of his office to the waiting room and said, "see you next Thursday.

CHAPTER TEN

It was Saturday, 10:30 in the morning and I was finishing up my tuna breakfast, it was the only thing I could prepare with the little energy I felt I had when I heard a knock on the door. "Althea, hi," Crawfard said as I opened the door, "oh-- hi-- I--am I confused, and is it already Thursday?" I said, he laughed, "no, but I said you should go out more and I felt like even if I had told you, you still wouldn't." he continued, "so go on, run on and do a quick change. we're going fishing." We drove about 15 minutes away from my house, I had packed my tote bag with my notebook, sketchbook, pens, and the current book I had been reading. "You didn't have to bring all that," Crawfard said as he focused on the road, "You'll have so much fun fishing and learning to fish, it's peaceful." I just looked out the window. We arrived at the lake, he opened the back of his car and handed me these heavy fisherman overalls. They felt like silicone. "Put it on over your clothes, we'll be standing in the water to fish," he said I couldn't believe I was fishing after I had laughed and hearted so many memes about people who fished from Tiktok and Instagram. We head over to the lake and soon the water was up to my waist, the noise of the lake was peaceful as it streamed beyond me. Crawfard taught me the basics and techniques and said that we had to stay still but we could chat. "How are you feeling?' he asked I knew he would ask that, he always did like some broken record. "I feel confused, why am I here?" "You have to experience things, go out and not lock yourself up the way your mind already feels" "I could go out on my own", I said. "You would have continued in your old habits. This won't be a weekly thing. I just thought this would be a good way to talk, yknow, not focus on making eye contact but rather what we catch" he said. After speaking for a few minutes, he finally asked me again, "How do you feel?" "I feel peaceful." I really did, there was something about standing in moving water or still water that made me feel so safe and peaceful but I've always felt connected to the water, maybe it has to do with my zodiac. I'm a cancer. but that day I had ranted and talked to Crawfard way more than i would have ever in his little office. Like a dragon breathing words of anger, pain, and frustration. I trusted him. I wanted to continue therapy

CHAPTER ELEVEN

I sat downtown were some important people bustled around with their suitcases and mixed in with the hobos who were hallucinating at every corner of the street. How artistic I thought. The best of both worlds, both of those groups of people, crazy and brainwashed. One brainwashed by society and the other by drugs. I was downtown because there was a bookstore that sold secondhand books and had a grand variety of books way more than any thrift store, plus they also had a free hot cocoa bar. I was able to get my hands on a Frankenstein book and a Hannibal book. both amazing thrillers. I had read Frankenstein many times in school and I had only watched Hannibal through media of a film and Tv series by NBC but I had read online, the book went deeper than the films or any adaptation of TV did, more Gorey, I guess. I continued to watch the people bustling around and thought about how they lived this life, 9 to 5 or overtime, and didn't ever stop and question it. They looked like programmed hamsters, running on the wheel of life set by society. I didn't want to be like them, I wanted freedom, creativity, and the ability to help people. I walked over to my therapist's office which around the corner. I waited in the same waiting room, the navy blue carpet, the smell of hand-sanitizer, and all the other things that come with his fancy office. "Althea, come in" Crawfard called me into his office. it had been a month of seeing him as my therapist and surely he helped because everything began to dehaze. I wanted this to be my last visit, I wanted no more. "How are we feeling today?" he asked but I had asked myself in my head before he did, he was predictable. "You know, I feel ok" I answered honestly. "Do you? Well, do you feel you could do ok without me? Are you ready to move forward in your life?" I stared at his handsome face, I did develop a little crush on him, he was a total dilf. "I feel like I know myself better, thanks to you". "I'll begin the process of interviewing you then", I answered each question honestly and very sure for the first time in a long time. "Well.. you seem well enough to me but my door is always open for you," Crawfard said with a smile, almost as if he were happy that he was able to screw my head back on. I'm sure he'd miss my pay. I smiled and thanked him for everything, as I walked out of that building--I stood with the world in front of me, inspired by Patti Smith and Sylvia Plath, I stepped into the world with motivation to be everything they were. An author, an artist, a good friend, and inspirational to younger people. I was finally moi, me, Althea. Again

www.ingramcontent.com/pod-product-compliance
Lightning Source LLC
Chambersburg PA
CBHW060949130726
48001CB00003B/1139